D1401869

Clowns and Dragons!

#3

Laurent Richard
illustrated by **Nicolas Ryser**
Translation: **Edward Gauvin**

Graphic Universe™ • Minneapolis

STORY BY LAURENT RICHARD
ILLUSTRATIONS BY NICOLAS RYSER
TRANSLATION BY EDWARD GAUVIN

FIRST AMERICAN EDITION PUBLISHED IN 2014 BY GRAPHIC UNIVERSE™.

PITRES ET DRAGONS! BY LAURENT RICHARD AND NICOLAS RYSER © BAYARD ÉDITIONS, 2011
COPYRIGHT © 2014 BY LERNER PUBLISHING GROUP, INC., FOR THE US EDITION

GRAPHIC UNIVERSE™
A DIVISION OF LERNER PUBLISHING GROUP, INC.
241 FIRST AVENUE NORTH
MINNEAPOLIS, MN 55401 USA

FOR READING LEVELS AND MORE INFORMATION,
LOOK UP THIS TITLE AT WWW.LERNERBOOKS.COM.

MAIN BODY TEXT SET IN CCWILDWORDS 8.5/10.5.
TYPEFACE PROVIDED BY FONTOGRAPHER.

LIBRARY OF CONGRESS CATALOGING-IN-PUBLICATION DATA

RICHARD, LAURENT, 1968-
    [PITRES ET DRAGONS! ENGLISH.]
    CLOWNS AND DRAGONS! / LAURENT RICHARD ; ILLUSTRATED BY NICOLAS RYSER ; TRANSLATION,
EDWARD GAUVIN. — FIRST AMERICAN EDITION.
        P.   CM. — (TAO, THE LITTLE SAMURAI ; #3)
    SUMMARY: TAO IS A FEARLESS SAMURAI APPRENTICE STUDYING TO BECOME A VIRTUOSO MARTIAL
ARTIST. BUT WHEN YOU'RE NATURALLY GOOD AT PRANKS, PRACTICAL JOKES, AND OTHER SILLY
ANTICS (INCLUDING TRYING TO TEACH KUNG FU MOVES TO THE BIG, LAZY CAT, BRUCE LEE), IT'S
HARD TO CONCENTRATE ON LEARNING HOW TO SLAY DRAGONS.
    ISBN 978-1-4677-2096-0 (LIB. BDG. : ALK. PAPER)
    ISBN 978-1-4677-2555-2 (EBOOK)
    1. GRAPHIC NOVELS. [1. GRAPHIC NOVELS. 2. MARTIAL ARTS—FICTION. 3. SAMURAI—FICTION.
 4. SCHOOLS—FICTION. 5. BEHAVIOR—FICTION.] I. RYSER, NICOLAS, ILLUSTRATOR. II. GAUVIN,
EDWARD, TRANSLATOR. III. TITLE.
PZ7.7.R5CL 2014
741.5'944—DC23   2013027734

MANUFACTURED IN THE UNITED STATES OF AMERICA
1 - VI - 12/31/13

NO ONE WILL SEE YOU WITH THIS CHAMELEON DISGUISE!

HUH! WOW!

NOW, GO TO SNOW'S DOJO AND BRING ME BACK THOSE SECRET BOOKS!

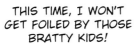

THIS TIME, I WON'T GET FOILED BY THOSE BRATTY KIDS!

I'LL SNEAK IN THE BACK WAY...

CAREFUL, THERE'S LOTS OF PEOPLE AROUND. LUCKILY I'M ALMOST INVISIBLE!

MASTER, I SWEAR OUR THREE ARROWS HIT THE TARGET!

YEAH, SURE...

UH-OH... I DON'T THINK I REMEMBER ALL THE CHOKEHOLDS ON THIS TEST!

NEXT!

HA! TOUGH LUCK, BUDDY. I'VE GOT A SUREFIRE LITTLE TRICK!

WHAT'S THAT?

YOU TAPED THE ANSWERS TO YOUR GI? THAT'S CHEATING!

IT'S NOT CHEATING. IT'S ADAPTING TO A HARD SITUATION!

NEXT!

SEE YA LATER!

WELL?

2 SLICES OF HAM, 2 POUNDS OF RICE, 1 BELL PEPPER, 3 TOMATOES...

HA HA HA

I TAPED ON MY GROCERY LIST!

4

Look Before You Leap

OVERSLEPT! I'M SO LATE!

I ALREADY MISSED HOMEROOM! GOTTA GET TO SWIM CLASS!

THE POOL STAIRS!

POOL

THE POOL LOCKER ROOM!

THE POOL SHOWERS!

PSCHII

AND THE POOL DIVING BOARD!

SBOUING

CLEANING

ONTO THE POOL FLOOR!

I CAN'T BELIEVE WHAT I'M HEARING, TUCK.

BUT IT'S TRUE!

RAY AND TAO ASKED YOU FOR MY PHOTO? IN MY CEREMONIAL ARMOR?

THAT'S RIGHT! I THINK THEY REALLY ADMIRE YOU!

AH, WHAT GOOD KIDS! AND HERE I THOUGHT THEY HATED MY CLASS.

I'M MOVED TO TEARS!

WHAT AN HONOR! A PHOTO IN MY STUDENTS' ROOM!

MAYBE I'LL DROP BY AND SAY HELLO!

KNOCK KNOCK!

UH...

YOU IN?

GULP!

TAO! TAO!

GULP!

DID I NOT TELL YOU TO WORK ON YOUR SHURIKEN* THROWING?

DID I NOT TELL YOU TO PRACTICE OUTSIDE CLASS?

ARE THESE THINGS NOT TRUE?

UH...YEAH...

BUT DID I TELL YOU TO PRACTICE IN THE CAFETERIA?

*SHURIKEN: THROWING STARS

The Little Samurai Is Like a Bamboo Shoot

IT WAS NICE OF YOU TO COME ON THIS LITTLE NATURE WALK WITH ME!

WELL, LEE SAID-- I MEAN, I THOUGHT YOU'D LIKE IT!

TEE HEE!

IT'S A NICE TIME OF YEAR FOR IT.

THE WEATHER'S WARM. WINTER'S OVER.

LITTLE FLOWERS ARE BLOOMING.

BIRDS ARE SINGING AGAIN.

AND BEARS ARE COMING OUT OF HIBERNATION!

THIS IS NOT GOING TO BE EASY!

YOU SAID IT, TAO!

MAN...

HMMMMM

THIS LESSON'S SUPER HARD! YOU STRESSED OUT ABOUT TODAY'S QUIZ TOO?

NO, NO!

IT'S JUST THAT THERE'S TWO LUNCH OPTIONS ON TODAY'S MENU. I CAN'T DECIDE BETWEEN SHRIMP DUMPLINGS AND SPICY BEEF!

MENU

Sugar Rush

MAN, YOU GUYS ARE REALLY LETTING ME DOWN!

I SWEAR, I READ IT ON THE INTERNET!

DON'T YOU WANT TO BE IN SHAPE FOR SATURDAY'S MATCH?

THE BODY NEEDS SUGAR TO KEEP A HIGH ENERGY LEVEL!

NOW WHO WANTS MORE GUMMI BEARS?

WEDNESDAY

ANYONE UP FOR CHOCOLATE?

I'M TELLING YOU--ENERGY!

THURSDAY

CANDY, KAT?

FRIDAY

THESE CHOCOLATE BARS ARE GONNA GET ME PUMPED UP FOR TOMORROW'S MATCH!

SATURDAY

DON'T WORRY-- JUST A BAD CASE OF INDIGESTION!

12

TAO! THIS IS A BAD START!

THIS IS THE THIRD TIME THIS MONTH YOU'VE FORGOTTEN YOUR TEXTBOOK!

LATER...

TAO, I DON'T WANT TO NAG YOU, BUT IT'S TRUE.

YOU COULD STAND TO BE A BIT MORE ORGANIZED.

WHY DON'T YOU TRY USING POST-IT NOTES TO REMIND YOU OF IMPORTANT STUFF?

BUT--

I DO THAT ALREADY!

LOOK!

Sculpture Comes Easy to a Samurai Master

BLOOPER! BLOOPER! THE TIME HAS COME!

MUUM MUUM

SNOW'S DOJO IS UNDER RENOVATION!

SNEAKING INTO THE LIBRARY WILL BE A PIECE OF CAKE!

GO ON! HURRY! BRING ME BACK THOSE SECRET TOMES!

ZIP

HEH HEH, THIS IS CHILD'S PLAY! NO ONE'S LOOKING TWICE!

OH NO! NO WAY!

ARE YOU OUT OF YOUR MIND? THERE'S NO PLAYING ON THE SCAFFOLDING!

FLAP FLP

MAN, I CAN'T CONCENTRATE WITH ALL THAT NOISE OUTSIDE OUR CLASSROOM!

EH...

WHEN YOU REALLY FOCUS, YOU CAN DROWN IT OUT.

STILL, IT BOTHERS ME!

I'M TELLING YOU: CONCENTRATION!

CRONTCH

CRONTCH

CRONTCH

CRONTCH

CRONTCH

CRONTCH

CRONTCH

WILL YOU GET OUT OF HERE! YOU CHEW SO LOUD, I CAN'T EVEN READ MY COMIC!

Cannonball!

IT'S TOO COLD FOR SWIMMING. AND TOO EARLY IN THE DAY!

NOT GONNA SWIM TODAY!

SORRY, MASTER, I'M FEELING UNDER THE WEATHER.

OK, TAO. STAY OUT OF THE WATER.

I'LL KEEP BACK TO AVOID GETTING SPLASHED.

PERFECT!

NOW, COMICS TIME!

HELP! THE SUMO WRESTLERS ARE COMING!

SPLASHH

PERRRFECT.

HA HA! LEFT THOSE FISHIES IN THE DUST!

WHO'S THE FLIPPER KING?

LEE, YOU CAN'T IMAGINE HOW FAST I WAS GOING!

MAN, I'M HUNGRY! COME DOWN FOR A SNACK WITH ME. I'LL TELL YOU ALL ABOUT IT!

SURE, BUT UH--

YOU SHOULD TAKE YOUR FLIPPERS OFF!

A Samurai Knows What He Wants

THIS YEAR I'VE GOT IT DOWN! NOT EVEN NOON YET, AND I'M READY FOR SCHOOL TOMORROW MORNING!

CAN'T WAIT TO SEE MY FRIENDS AGAIN: KAT, RAY, LEE...

QUICK CHECK: KATA MANUALS, NOTEBOOKS...

...KIMONOS, WOODEN WEAPONS...

MY PENCIL CASE. I EVEN WROTE OUT MY SCHEDULE.

I DIDN'T FORGET A--

NO, I DID. I JUST FORGOT THAT--

SCHOOL STARTS TODAY, NOT TOMORROW!

SIGH... I'M KINDA SICK OF ALL THE CONSTRUCTION AT SCHOOL.

I'M SURPRISED, LEE. YOU NEVER COMPLAIN!

PLUS, ALL THIS CONSTRUCTION'S A GOOD CHANCE TO TRAIN! WE CAN WORK...

ON STRENGTH!

ON AGILITY!

ON FLEXIBILITY AND BALANCE!

BLOM

ON CAMOUFLAGE?

YO YO YO! TAO'S CATCHING UP TO HIS COMPETITION!

IT'S CLEAR WHO THE BEST IS TODAY!

THE FASTEST! THE COOLEST!

SURE IT'S HARD! SURE IT HURTS! BUT HE'S STAYING RIGHT ON THEIR TAIL!

HE PUTS HIS ALL INTO IT! HE'S ABOUT TO PASS THEM!

LOOK, TAO, WE'RE IN A GYM. SO GO AS HARD AS YOU WANT...

...BUT DO IT QUIETLY!!

A Sixth Sense Shows the Way

WAIT A SEC! THE FOG'S GETTING THICKER!

SO WHAT?

LOOK, YOU WANNA GO TO THE LIBRARY? WE'LL GO TO THE LIBRARY, PEA SOUP OR NO.

A SAMURAI HAS A SUPERNATURAL SENSE OF DIRECTION!

MAYBE, BUT...

I REALLY CAN'T SEE A THING.

GRAB MY KIMONO! BE AWED BY THE WARRIOR WHO FINDS HIS WAY IN DARKEST NIGHT.

HERE WE ARE! IT'S CLEARING UP, TOO!

IT SMELLS WEIRD!

A Little Grasshopper Sure Can Be Loud

STOP IT! STOP FIGHTING AT ONCE!

I WARNED YOU! YOU CAN'T HAVE THE SLED IF YOU WON'T SHARE IT!

BUT THAT'S WHAT WE'RE DOING! KAT AND MIMI GET AS MUCH SLED TIME AS WE DO!

THEN WHAT'S THE PROBLEM?

OF COURSE! WE GET IT GOING UPHILL, AND THEY GET IT GOING DOWN!

ARE THEY LYING, KAT?

TAO! I THINK I FOUND IT! LET'S SEE...ARTICLE 59B OF THE SCHOOL CODE.

YES! HERE IT IS!

IN CASE OF SNOW, SOME AREAS OF THE SCHOOL ARE FORBIDDEN.

GIVEN THE NATURE OF THE GROUNDS, THESE AREAS ARE DANGEROUS.

VERY LOCALIZED AVALANCHES MAY OCCUR.

THAT IS WHY--

OK, LEE, YOU WERE RIGHT! NOW HELP ME OUT OF HERE!

Mirror, Mirror on the Wall

WELL, THIS TIME THERE'S NO DOUBTING IT!

TAO IS THE CHAMPION OF THE WORLD!

TCHACK

THE BIGGEST! THE STRONGEST! THE HANDSOMEST!

SLURP SLURP

Y'KNOW, BRUCE LEE, I'M IN GREAT SHAPE! CHECK OUT THESE GUNS!

FROT FROT

...

FF FF FF PFF FF

SIGH... SOME GUYS JUST LIVE TO SHOW OFF...

HEY, TAO!

DECKING THE PINE TREES WITH ARROWS? NEAT IDEA!

FESTIVE...AND ORIGINAL!

WHAT ARE YOU TALKING ABOUT?

I'M JUST PRACTICING MY ARCHERY, THAT'S ALL!

OH...

TAO, YOU REALLY HAVE TO STOP PRACTICING MOVES IN THE CAFETERIA!

PLEASE! IT'S GETTING ANNOYING!

AAAYAA!

CRAACK

I MEAN, IT'S OK WITH THE CRACKERS.

BUT--

AAYAA

CALIFORNIA ROLLS ARE ANOTHER STORY!

WONDERFUL!

THE STUDENTS DID A GREAT JOB THIS YEAR.

THIS ICE SCULPTING COMPETITION IS A TERRIFIC IDEA!

HEH. THIS TAO STATUE'S REALLY GOOD!

IT SURE IS! DO YOU THINK IT'S A SELF-PORTRAIT?

HURRY, HURRY! HE WAS FROZEN SOLID WHEN I PULLED HIM OUT OF THE POND!

GNN

A Loving Cry

THIS IS GREAT, TAO! YOU HAVE A LITTLE BROTHER!

YEAH, WAIT TILL YOU SEE HIM! HE'S WAY CUTE!

OOP! I FORGOT THE ROOM NUMBER!

HUH?

DON'T WORRY. I'LL JUST CALL HIM.

TAO, NO!

RELAX! HE'LL TOTALLY RECOGNIZE HIS BROTHER'S VOICE!

YOOO HOOO! NEEOOO!

IT'S TAO!

Flying High on Dragon's Wings

HAH! LOOK AT THOSE GUYS. THEY THINK THEY'RE SO TOUGH!

AYAH BLAM

YEAH, NOT BAD. BUT FAR FROM THE BEST!

C'MON, GUYS! PUT YOUR BACK INTO IT.

EVEN I COULD BEAT YOU IF I WANTED.

UM... TAO? LET'S GO!

SURE, LEE. LET'S HIT THE BIG-BOY RIDES AND GIVE THE GIRLY MEN PRACTICE TIME.

JUST HURRY UP!

WHOOHOOOO!

NOW THIS IS A REAL RIDE!

BUT TAO--

WHAT'S THE MATTER, LEE? TOO SCARED TO MAKE A SOUND?

NO, IT'S JUST... YOUR SEAT BELT'S NOT BUCKLED!

OH, RIGHT...

HIIIII

WHOA, DUDE... RESPECT!

BLAM

GNNAARG...

A Samurai's Modest Gifts

NO WAY! I MISSED AGAIN! THESE STUPID BALLOONS WON'T STOP MOVING!

I'M GOING AGAIN! I WANT TO WIN SOMETHING FOR KAT!

NOPE!

URRGHH!

MISSED AGAIN!

HUH?

IT'S GOOD! HERE'S A LITTLE STUFFED ANIMAL, YOUNG MAN. SEE YA LATER! NEXT!

YES!

KA--

YES?

UH... FORGET IT!

Book Learning Is Easy on the Ear

. . . what matters most in a kata is spirit. Rhythm; stances, whether low, high . . .

. . . or sustained; and all our inner human qualities. Also keenness of vision, mental focus from beginning to end, and total physical concentration reinforcing . . . *

WHOA! VERY IMPRESSIVE, TAO!

MY SON, STUDYING HIS BOOKS! WHAT A RARE SIGHT!

WEEEELL . . .

THIS WAS THE ONLY THING THAT PUT NEO TO SLEEP. WHEN I STOP READING, HE CRIES!

ZZZ ZZZ

*HENRY PLÉE, KARATE BLACK BELT

Flying Off the Handle

HEY...

WHAA--? RAY, WHAT HAPPENED TO YOU?

I WAS IN THE PARK. THERE WERE FLIES EVERYWHERE...

LISTEN TO YOURSELF! FLIES CAN'T DO THAT TO YOU!

YEAH! A BEAR, MAYBE, BUT NOT FLIES!

NO, IT WASN'T THEM. SOMEONE ELSE WAS IN THE PARK TOO.

TAO!

STUPID BUGS!

?

Grasshopper, Listen to Your Elders

TUT-TUT! YOUR STANCES LACK CONVICTION. YOU MUST APPLY YOURSELF, YOUNG TAO!

THINK ABOUT YOUR BREATHING! IT'S VERY IMPORTANT.

SURE, SURE!

BUT, GRANDPA, YOU HAVEN'T DONE KARATE IN AT LEAST A CENTURY!

OK, SEE YOU LATER! GOING TO MEET UP WITH RAY.

DON'T FORGET YOUR UMBRELLA, TAO!

YEAH, SURE!

GRANDPARENTS ALWAYS HAVE TO GET THE LAST WORD! WITH ALL THEIR OLD-FASHIONED ADVICE...

YEAH... FUNNY...

The True Test of a Samurai

GOOD, RAY!

WOW! YOU LOST EVERY FIGHT THIS MORNING, BUT YOU KEPT YOUR TEMPER.

THAT'S RIGHT! TODAY NOTHING AND NO ONE CAN BREAK MY COOL.

TODAY'S A VERY SPECIAL DAY: THE SEASON FINALE OF SAMURAI KIVAO.

NO TEARS, NO SHOUTING, NO TANTRUMS. I'M WAY TOO EXCITED.

WAIT, YOU HAVEN'T HEARD THE NEWS?

THE TV IN THE LOUNGE IS BROKEN!

The Great Ninja Knows (Almost) No Fear

YAH!

YAH!

GOO!

SEE, NEO? NINJAS ARE AWESOME WARRIORS! THE DEADLIEST FIGHTERS!

AT NIGHT, THEY TIPTOE ACROSS THE ROOFTOPS...

...TOTALLY INVISIBLE! EXPERTS AT CAMOUFLAGE!

THEY USE POISON DARTS OR SWORDS OR DAGGERS! THEY FEAR NO ONE!

TAO! CLEAN UP THIS MESS RIGHT NOW!

UH...EXCEPT THEIR MOTHERS!

Lightning-Fast Reflexes

太閤記
銘々傳
二篇

朝香樓
芳春筆

47

TOSS THE BAGS IN!

TAO! WHERE ARE YOU?

POF

52

I'M VERY DISAPPOINTED, CHILDREN.

LAST NIGHT, THE TRASH BAGS WERE EMPTIED IN FRONT OF THE PROFESSORS' DOORS!

YIKES! HE GOT THE WRONG DOOR!

ULP!

AND THAT SAME NIGHT, CHOCOLATE PUDDING WAS STOLEN FROM THE CAFETERIA! THIS NONSENSE WILL NOT BE TOLER--UH-OH.

SINCE THE GUILTY PARTIES WERE SO EASY TO SPOT, I WON'T KEEP EVERYONE ANY LONGER. MASTER IRONS?

TAO! RAY! MY OFFICE!

NO WAY! HOW'D YOU KNOW?

53

Get ready for the next
books in the Tao, the
Little Samurai series!

THE CHAMPIONSHIP!

When two top students from Master Snow's school disappear,
Tao and his friends are on the case! This book-length Tao
adventure has mysteries, a clan of nasty criminals, and a hunt
for a legendary sword!

WILD ANIMALS!

A new student has arrived at Master Snow's school—and
she has a crush on Tao! Meanwhile, Tao is teaching his little
brother how to take care of bullies. He's also teaching his
cat some ninja attacks!

#1 Pranks and Attacks!
#2 Ninjas and Knock Outs!
#3 Clowns and Dragons!